The
Seaside Bears

The Colonel   Theo

Koala Lumpa   MacLavender   Tubbytoes

The
Ironbridge Bears

Martha   Mortimer   Max

Marigold

For Kathy, Seán and Gemma

The Ironbridge bears featured in this book are made by
Merrythought Ltd., Ironbridge, Shropshire.

First published in 1992 by
Uplands Books
1 The Uplands, St Leonards,
East Sussex TN38 0HL

Text and illustrations copyright © 1992 Prue Theobalds

ISBN 0 9512246 5 4 pbk
ISBN 0 9512246 6 2 bound

*Printed in Hong Kong by
Dai Nippon Printing Company (H. K.) Ltd.*

The Bears' Seaside Adventure

by
Prue Theobalds

Uplands Books

One summer morning a postcard landed on the doormat.
Theo picked it up and just managed to read:
   "Dear Cousins . . . ."
before the Colonel, who always liked to think he was in charge,
bustled up to him and said, "Let me see that!"

The Colonel put on his glasses and read:
"Dear Cousins at the seaside,
We are coming to stay with you because
We fancy a holiday by the sea,
See you soon,
    Mortimer, Martha,
        Marigold and Max"

"Who are Mortimer, Martha, Marigold and Max?" asked Tubbytoes.

"They come from a place called Ironbridge," said Koala Lumpa, who had been studying the picture on the other side of the postcard.

"Where's that?" asked Theo.

"It is a place where everything is made from Meccano," said the Colonel, pretending he knew all about it.

POSTCARD

Dear Cousins
at the Seaside
we are comming
with

The Seaside Bears
1 The Uplands
Maze Hill
St. Leonards
E. Sussex

"Are they made of Meccano too?" asked Tubbytoes in a rather worried voice.

"We shall have to wait and see," said Theo.

"Well, they cannae sleep on my piece of the windysill," muttered McLavender in his usual grumpy voice.

A few days later, when Theo was busy inventing a new, very special kind of kite, the Ironbridge bears arrived. Theo was not pleased to be interrupted, but the rest of the seaside bears clustered inquisitively round the new arrivals, and were relieved to see that they were not made of metal, but of fur just like themselves.

There was Mortimer, who looked rather absent-minded but seemed to be in charge; Martha, who wore an apron and looked as though she might fuss around them; Marigold, the smallest bear, who looked, at first sight, as if she would be as good as gold, but had the kind of smile that made you think otherwise; and Max, who looked shy and friendly and was eyeing Theo's kite with great interest.

The seaside bears, apart from McLavender, found the Ironbridge bears friendly and fun to be with and it was not long before they were treating them like old friends.

Within a few days, Theo and Max had finished making the kite and were longing to try it out. The Colonel, who liked to organise expeditions, decided to arrange a trip to the beach, with a grand picnic lunch as the highlight.

Koala Lumpa and Tubbytoes, who were both extremely
interested in food, volunteered to help Martha prepare the
picnic. The Colonel made a great many lists and consulted a
few maps. In fact, everyone was busy except for McLavender
who sulked in the background and said it was too cold for
swimming.

The bears found a large hamper and packed into it everything they thought they might need: bathing costumes, towels, buckets and spades, rugs, sun hats, an umbrella (just in case!), lots of food and plenty of nice fizzy drinks.

A strange procession made its way down to the beach. The Colonel led the way, carrying a large pair of binoculars, then came Koala Lumpa and Mortimer, struggling with the hamper, and Martha and Tubbytoes with their arms full of towels. Theo and Max were carefully carrying the kite, and Marigold, who was fascinated by the kite but had not been allowed to touch it, carried the string.

McLavender followed, some distance behind, wearing a pair of green plastic sunglasses and pretending that he had nothing to do with the party.

They climbed down onto the beach, found a spot that was neither too pebbly nor too sandy, and spread themselves out.

The bears changed into their bathing things. Mortimer stretched out on a sandy piece of beach with a towel over his head and was soon snoring loudly. Koala Lumpa and Tubbytoes started to dig a sandcastle nearby, and when no one was looking they shovelled sand on Mortimer's feet.

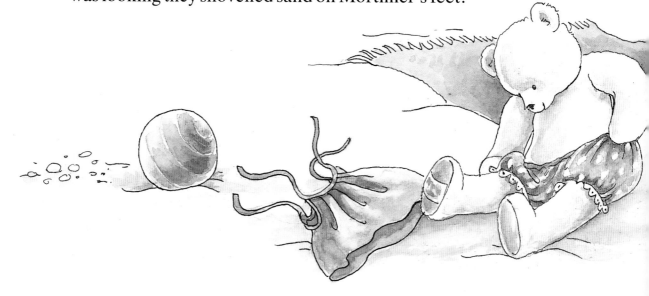

Theo and Max tried to get the kite ready for flying, but got themselves tied in knots. Martha busied herself with the contents of the hamper and McLavender sat some distance away – just close enough to keep one beady eye on the hamper.

Soon Mortimer's feet had disappeared from view and there was a pile of sand on his tummy with a sandcastle on top. No one seemed to notice because all eyes were on the kite which was now ready for its first flight.

Marigold saw the kite was about to be launched and came rushing over, calling out, "Let me hold the string! You said I could be in charge of the string!"

She grabbed the end of the string just as the wind caught the kite. Before any of them knew what was happening, both the kite and Marigold were high in the air. They looked up in shocked silence, wondering what to do.

Marigold's frightened squeaks were getting fainter and they realized, with horror, that the kite was now over the water.

At that moment, a small figure in tartan bathing trunks came running from the back of the beach.

"Let go o' the string, lassie! Jump!" he shouted.
"McLavender will catch you."

"Jump, Marigold!" shouted all the rest of the bears.

Marigold shut her eyes and jumped.

There was a big splash. Then they saw, with relief,
McLavender with Marigold in his arms wading out of the sea.
Theo and Max ran in to help while Koala Lumpa tried to wipe
the spray from his glasses and sort out what was happening.

At last they were all safely on the beach and Martha had wrapped them in dry towels. The Colonel did a quick head count to see if everyone was accounted for . . . . and discovered that Mortimer was missing.

"Where is Mortimer?"

"He must have drowned," sobbed Martha.

Then, to their relief, they saw the large mound of sand with the sand castle on top give a shudder and Mortimer emerged rubbing his eyes.

"I must have dozed off," he said sleepily. "Have I missed the picnic?"

They could not believe that he had slept through all the excitement. Theo tried to explain what had happened.

"I nearly disappeared for ever," squealed Marigold.

"I expect my kite is now somewhere over France," said Theo wistfully.

"Don't worry," said Max kindly, "we will make another one."

McLavender was the hero of the hour. Martha kissed him on both cheeks, much to his embarrassment.

"Och, it was nae bother," he muttered, looking rather pink. "It's given me an appetite, though. I reckon I could just manage a wee bit o' Martha's picnic after all."